Lemon Bird was penciled, inked,
colored, and lettered in Photoshop.

Text, cover art, and interior illustrations copyright © 2022 by Paulina Ganucheau

All rights reserved. Published in the United States by RH Graphic, an imprint of
Random House Children's Books, a division of Penguin Random House LLC, New York.

RH Graphic with the book design is a trademark of Penguin Random House LLC.

Visit us on the web! RHKidsGraphic.com • @RHKidsGraphic

Educators and librarians, for a variety of teaching tools, visit us at RHTeachersLibrarians.com

Library of Congress Cataloging-in-Publication Data is available upon request.
ISBN 978-0-593-12267-9 (hardcover) — ISBN 978-0-593-12533-5 (lib. bdg.)
ISBN 978-0-593-12268-6 (ebook)

Designed by Patrick Crotty

MANUFACTURED IN CHINA
10 9 8 7 6 5 4 3 2 1
First Edition

A comic on every bookshelf.

LEMON BIRD

BIRD

Can Help!

Paulina
Ganucheau

To Mamaw and Papaw

3

7

27

42

BOING

PIP

67

WE'RE COMING, PUPKIN!!

95

Acknowledgments

So many thanks to give! First, I want to thank Gina Gagliano, for this book would not exist without her query for more *Lemon Bird*. You saw the potential this little citrus bird had even before I did!

My agent, Charlie Olsen, for being the rock-star guiding-hand businessman who always gets my projects going on the right track. Same to my editor Whitney Leopard and my designer Patrick Crotty!

Mamaw and Papaw. You both gave me so many beautiful memories of creativity, fun, and laughter that I still carry with me to this day. It was so fitting that I was at your house when I found out *Lemon Bird* the graphic novel was being acquired. This book is for you both.

To my whole family. Mama and Daddo, I love you! Savi, my bestie comics sister. Kendall, my partner and my best pal. You keep me going. To all my friends, Kevin, Door, Julian, Coleman, Patrick, Robyn, Emily, Brad, Jess, Gabe, Tory. Thank you for cheering me on!

My supporters. My fans. To anyone who ever said my art brought them joy. I create for you. ♥

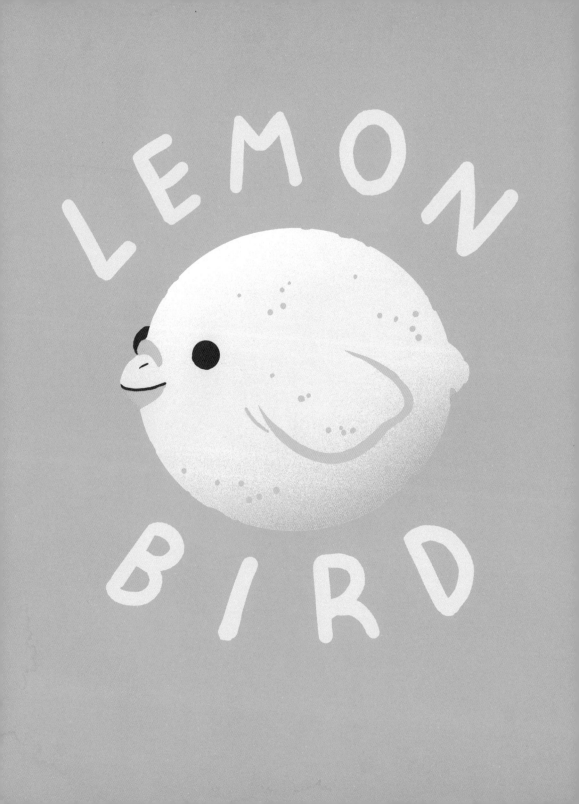

HOW TO DRAW LEMON BIRD!

STEP 1: DRAW A CIRCLE.
(DOESN'T HAVE TO BE PERFECT!)

STEP 2: LET'S ADD SOME LITTLE FLIPPERS FOR HER WINGS!

STEP 3: STACK TWO LITTLE TRIANGLES ON TOP OF EACH OTHER FOR HER BEAK.

STEP 4: ADD THE SMALL FACE DETAILS AND YOU'RE DONE! SHE'S READY TO FLY!

KEYLIME

SIZE
COMPARISON

PEACH

Here are some Fruit Animal
mix-ups! What fruit and animal
would you combine?

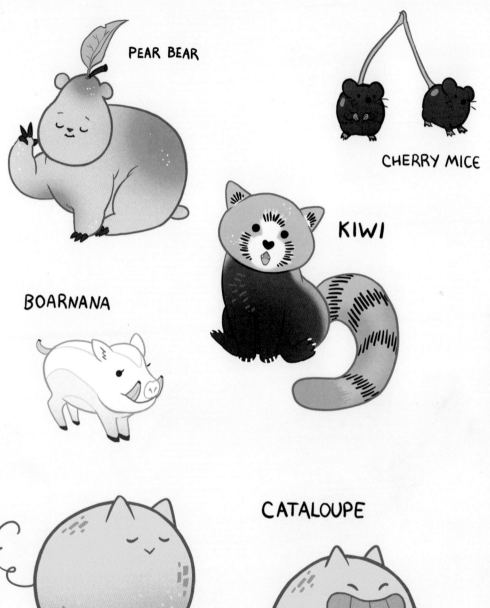

PEAR BEAR

CHERRY MICE

KIWI

BOARNANA

CATALOUPE

Paulina Ganucheau is an artist who lives in Virginia with her dog and two cats. She grew up in New Orleans, where she and her sister would make comics together. She's been drawing ever since. Paulina attended art college in Georgia and has been published by many companies, including Marvel, DC, and Scholastic. A few of her other books are *Zodiac Starforce*, *She-ra: Legend of the Fire Princess*, and *Wonder Woman: The Adventures of Young Diana*. *Lemon Bird* started off as a fun little joke, but soon turned into a passion project. The idea came from a calendar Paulina had of vintage scientific illustrations. One particular month was of a parrot sitting next to a lemon, and thus *Lemon Bird* was born. Besides drawing, some of her hobbies include watching pro wrestling, cloud photography, and following dogs on Instagram.

AWESOME COMICS!
AWESOME KIDS!

Introduce your youngest reader to comics with

RH **GRAPHIC**

📷 🐦 **@RHKidsGraphic** A graphic novel on every bookshelf

RHCB